BRITTLE

FOR THE

MAGICALLY UNSTABLE

Charlie Makes a Discovery!

By

Lily Mae Walters

Cover design by Mia Romano

Illustrated by Tom Rowley

Edited by Denna Holm

Publisher's Publication in Data

Walters, Lily Mae

Brittle's Academy for the Magically Unstable

1. Juvenile Fiction 2. Mystery 3. Paranormal 4. Magic

Welcome to the first in the series of *Brittle's Academy for the Magically Unstable*. The books can be read and enjoyed in any order as long as you've read *Charlie Makes a Discovery* first, which introduces us to the magical world of Professor Brittle, his pupils, the teachers and, of course, the school.

Coming soon to the Brittle series:

Maisey takes a tumble
Harry takes a test
Phoebe makes a mess
Taylor teaches the class
Professor Peculiar loses her grace
Professor Brittle goes on a quest
Mia paints a picture
Sandeep to the rescue

For Ben

Who believed in all things magical. A beautiful empathic soul who loved to pass the smile to people to make them feel better. Chief maker of mischief. Stolen too early. Forever 7.

And for James and Harry, his big brothers.

CHAPTER 1

Charlie stared at the crisply ironed uniform hanging on his wardrobe door. The black blazer with its golden lion badge was at least two sizes too big for him but his mum had insisted he would 'grow into it'. The pristine white shirt with its stiff, uncomfortable collar peeped out from underneath along with the black and yellow tie which he had just learnt to tie properly the previous evening.

He longed for his junior school days when a polo shirt and jumper were the order of the day. Easy, comfortable clothes you could play football or climb trees in, but Charlie had already been warned by his mother, forbidden to get even the smallest rip or tear in any of his new uniform as it had cost a small fortune.

"I don't know why you can't wear your cousin's blazer," his mum had argued when he brought home the list of everything he'd need for his new school on the last day of term.

"Because she's a girl," he replied, mortified his mum even considered that to be an option.

"It's only the button that's on the other side," she insisted. "No one will even notice." She picked up her mobile phone. "I'll text your Auntie Jean now and ask her to drop it down tomorrow."

"You will do no such thing." Charlie's big brother Alex came into the room at this precise moment, much to Charlie's relief. Technically, he was Charlie's half-brother as they had different dads but neither of them cared very much about this.

Alex was ten years older and worked at the local garage where he'd been an apprentice from the age of sixteen. He'd worked his way up and was already head mechanic. Charlie quite often went to work with him in the holidays and loved tinkering about with the engines or pretending he was a racing car driver at Silverstone.

"He can wear your old ones then," his mum said, plonking her phone down with an angry thump. "I'm sure I've kept them upstairs somewhere."

"Charlie is half the size I was at that age," Alex protested.

"Then I'll have to get Maureen down the road to take them in." She flung open the door and stomped up the stairs.

"Don't worry, little bro." Alex ruffled Charlie's brown hair affectionately at the despondent look in his eyes. "I'll get you everything you need."

Charlie hugged him tightly.

"And a brand-new bag, lunch box, anything you want." This had earned him another hug. "Can't have a brother of mine turning up for school in hand-me-downs now, can we?"

So Alex took the day off work and, along with his girlfriend Chloe, took Charlie to the school wear centre in the middle of town. Afterwards, they treated Charlie to a slap-up lunch at the American diner: chocolate milkshakes, the biggest cheeseburger Charlie had ever seen and a fudge brownie for dessert, all soft and gooey inside.

Unfortunately, upon their return home—and after having examined the purchases—their mother had insisted on exchanging the blazer for a larger one.

"There's no point getting him one that fits now," she'd said. "He'll have grown at least an inch before the end of summer, and then they won't take it back. And I'm not forking out for new shoes either. Your old ones will do just fine."

To save arguments, Chloe returned the blazer the next day and handed Charlie the larger size. However, he didn't grow an inch over the summer; he didn't even grow half an inch. In fact, he was pretty sure he'd shrunk. When he tried on the blazer the next week, it had practically covered his hands instead of ending nicely just over his wrist. He felt positive his mum had exchanged it for an even bigger size—always one to want her money's worth.

"Charlie!" his mother screeched up the stairs. "You'd best be out of bed, my lad. I won't have a son of mine late for school."

"Be down in a minute." He knew better than to linger in bed on a school morning and within five minutes he was washed and dressed and eating corn flakes washed down with a mug of milk.

"I'm leaving in five minutes, Charlie, if you want a lift," Alex said, walking into the living room from the kitchen.

"He's perfectly capable of walking, you know," his mum said. "I walked five miles to school every day come rain or shine."

"We know you did, Mum." Alex rolled his eyes at Charlie, which made him giggle. "But it's his first day and I've borrowed Mr Hunter's Jag specially."

"Really?" Charlie's eyes widened. Mr Hunter was the owner of the garage that Alex worked at. He had a fleet of vintage cars. "The blue one?"

"Yep, the blue one." Alex nodded, jangling keys in front of him.

"You spoil that boy," their mum said before she stormed into the kitchen where they could hear her angrily washing plates.

"We'll see you later," Alex called out, receiving a disgruntled 'humph' in reply.

It was only a five-minute drive to Park Hill Secondary, but in all the school traffic it took three times as long, and Charlie didn't mind one bit. He quite enjoyed sitting back in the cream leather seats, watching the world go by.

"Can we do this every morning?" he asked Alex as they pulled up outside the school gates.

"I'm afraid not, little bro." Alex pulled on the handbrake. "Just this once for your first day."

Charlie's face fell at the sight of all the other children heading into school.

"You'll be okay, you know," Alex reassured. "Your friends from primary school will be in there. In fact, isn't that Jack now?" Alex pointed to a red car that had pulled up in front of them.

"It's not that, Alex." Charlie turned to look at him. "I'm just not sure which entrance to go through."

"There's only one gate, Charlie." Alex looked at his brother, his expression confused. "Those ones just there." He nodded in the direction of the school sign where two grey gates stood wide open.

"What about that wooden one there?" Charlie pointed. "I've just seen two boys go through it."

"Are you feeling okay?" Alex asked, concerned. "There's no wooden gate."

"Hey, Charlie." A knock on the window showed Jack's beaming face grinning at him through the glass. "The bell's about to go."

"See you later, Alex." Charlie opened the door and joined his friend on the pavement.

Alex waved cheerily, apparently putting the conversation about a second gate out of his head.

"Can you believe we're seniors?" Jack said as they joined the crowds of other pupils milling towards the gates.

"Why are they wearing a different uniform?" Charlie watched a taller girl and boy walk past him in the opposite direction. "Are they prefects? Is that the prefects' entrance?"

"What you on about, Charlie?" Jack looked around. "Everyone's got the same uniform on."

"Those two behind us." Charlie turned around. The tall boy had opened the gate to allow the girl through, then just before he disappeared through it himself, he looked straight at Charlie and pressed his finger to his lips in a shushing motion. The door shimmered and disappeared as soon as the boy closed it.

CHAPTER 2

"Good morning, year sevens." Charlie, Jack and the rest of the new pupils had filed into the school theatre for a welcome assembly. Six teachers sat in plastic chairs behind a wooden podium. Above the podium was a bun of tight grey hair that appeared to be floating. "Quiet now." The bun spoke in a posh accent and Charlie could just see black shoes peeping out from underneath. "I am Mrs Martell, head teacher here at Park Hill Secondary."

"My sister says she's a right battle axe," Jack whispered to Charlie behind his hand.

"Your form tutors are all here behind me and we are looking forward to helping you become the best you can be in your next five years here at Park Hill Secondary." The bun stepped out from behind the podium to reveal the tiniest woman Charlie had ever seen. She was dressed in a frilly white shirt and a dark blue jacket and skirt. Charlie was sure she must have had this specially made because she couldn't have been much more than four feet tall.

"I'm Mr Jones." One of the teachers stood up. He had curly brown hair and wore a yellow shirt tucked into brown trousers with a brown tie. "If I call your name, please stand up and make your way to the back of the theatre." He started calling out names, and one by one pupils stood up and moved. Friends waited eagerly to see if they would be picked to be in the same form. "Follow me, 7J." The line of thirty children followed Mr Jones out as another teacher stood up to take his place.

"My name is Mrs Leech." Whether it was the contrast of standing near to Mrs Martell or whether Mrs Leech was just extremely tall, but she towered over most of her students by at least a foot as she led them away.

The fifth teacher was calling out names now, and so far Charlie and Jack were still seated on wooden benches.

"Jack Roberts."

Charlie watched as Jack stood up and gave him a reassuring smile. He started muttering Charlie Woods over and over willing his name to be called so he might be in the same form as his best friend.

"Follow me, 7K."

Charlie watched Jack walk out and looked around.

There was still well over thirty pupils dotted around; in fact, he was sure he counted at least forty, if not more. Was this one teacher to have all of them in one group? He knew his mum would have a field day with this. 'Oversubscribed schools,' she would say. 'How are children expected to learn in crowded classrooms?' And her favourite saying of all, which she used for virtually anything, 'I don't know what they spend our taxes on.'

The last teacher, Mrs Bacon, stood up and started to call names from her list. Charlie noticed Tasha Boyle look a little confused as Mrs Bacon was now calling a pupil with a surname of Farmer. The same look crossed Edward Gregory's face as she moved onto Joshua Jones. Then Sandeep Keer was missed out, and Charlie saw two pupils he didn't know exchange worried glances and presumed they had been forgotten as well.

"Right then, 7B."

Surely this isn't right, Charlie thought to himself, shrugging at Phoebe Robinson and Alide Valberga, who were looking nervously around.

Mrs Bacon teetered down the steps of the stage in her incredibly thin high heels which clip clopped as she walked towards the back.

Mrs Martell, looking rather bewildered, said, "Erm..." She stepped back behind the podium. "Well then, children, I'm not quite sure what's happened here. I'll have to get Mrs Glover in admissions to have a look over all the lists. If you just wait here for a moment." She hurried off the stage and out of the theatre much faster than Charlie thought her capable of.

"What's going on?" Sandeep stepped over a few of the benches to sit next to Charlie. The others following suit till all fifteen of them were seated in a small group near the front. "They can't have missed us all off the list, surely?"

"I was definitely down on the class list when we visited for open day," Phoebe said.

"And me," Alide agreed.

"I could see them getting one or two wrong but not half a class," Charlie piped in.

They chatted for a few minutes before Mrs Martell came back followed by an extremely flustered looking woman who Charlie assumed was Mrs Glover.

"Every year," Mrs Martell whispered angrily. "It's happened every year since this school was opened. How can we miss fifteen children? It was twenty-two last year, eighteen the year before."

"I don't know, Mrs Martell." Mrs Glover searched frantically through her papers. "I counted them ten times to make sure, honestly, I did. We had 192 pupils for the year with 32 in each form."

"So what happened?" Mrs Martell started counting the names in each form. "Not one of these has 32 names. Three have 30, and three have 29, so that's…" Charlie watched her pause as she calculated the sum in her head. "That's the missing 15." She almost threw the papers back at Mrs Glover, scowling. For such a little woman she was very intimidating, and Charlie vowed to never get in her bad books. "Well then, children…" She started to step on the stage. "…it seems there's been a little clerical error."

"No error, Mrs Martell." Everyone turned at the male voice, but no one could actually see him in the room. "I altered the lists as I do every year."

"Professor Brittle, of course." Mrs Martell's whole demeanour changed. "How lovely to see you again. Did you have a good summer? I'm so sorry, Mrs Glover must have forgotten your class list."

"I had a fabulous summer, thank you." The male voice seemed to hang in the air, but Charlie still couldn't see who it actually belonged to. "I'm sure my class list is right there."

Mrs Glover began searching again. "But … I'm sure…" She pulled out a piece of gold paper. "I know that wasn't there a minute ago."

"I'll leave you with your class, Professor Brittle." And with that, Mrs Martell ushered the confused and sobbing Mrs Glover out of the theatre.

"Good morning, class." The voice from the back of the room was now coming from the stage. Charlie and the other children turned back to face the front, where a cloud of gold-coloured smoke had started to form. "I hope you're ready for an exciting day." As they stared at the smoke, it started to whirl and disappear, leaving behind a tall, smartly dressed man. "Wonderful to meet you all. I'm Professor Brittle."

CHAPTER 3

Charlie wasn't sure if he was more in awe of the gentleman who now stood before them or of the way he had appeared.

The gold smoke had seemed to mould and shape itself, first turning into shiny, lace-up black shoes, followed by grey pinstripe trousers. Next came a grey pinstripe waistcoat which covered a pristine white shirt and a dark grey tie. Black-rimmed glasses were folded and tucked onto the top of the waistcoat, and a gold chain was clipped onto the hem, disappearing into one of the pockets.

The long brown coat came next, smoothed onto the shoulders, and fell almost to the floor. His face was the last thing to form. A very short and neatly trimmed beard framed a chiselled chin. A large but perfectly proportioned nose stood prominently in the middle, just a little wonky on one side. Kind brown eyes looked around, as if seeing them all for the first time, and short brown hair stood slightly quiffed to one side.

"Now I'm sure you are all wondering what's going on and who on earth I am?" He spoke in a deep voice as he clicked his fingers, and the gold sheet of paper that Mrs Glover had left with magically appeared in his hands. "As I'm sure you all heard, I'm Professor Brittle, head teacher here at Brittle's Academy."

He continued to talk, but no one was listening as they had all suddenly started whispering.

"Please, sir?" One of the boys Charlie didn't know stuck up his hand.

"Yes, Martin?" Professor Brittle smiled. "How can I help?"

"What do you mean by Brittle's Academy?" This had been the question everyone wanted answering. "We thought we were at Park Hill Secondary."

"And so you are, Martin." He stepped down from the stage and came to stand in front of them, and now Charlie could see how incredibly tall he was. Not too tall that he would have to bend to get through a doorway but tall enough to attract attention everywhere he went.

"So why did you say you're the head of Brittle's Academy?" Teddy Johnson butted in.

"Because I am, Teddy," he replied simply and without further explanation.

"How do you know my name?" Teddy looked warily at him.

"He's got a list, Dumbo," Alide teased.

"Still doesn't explain how he knew his name," Sandeep teased back.

"I've never met him so how would he know that Teddy is me."

"Same here," the boy called Martin quipped. "I've never met him, but he knew I was Martin."

"I know all of your names." They all jumped as Professor Brittle's voice now came from behind them. "And the faces they belong to."

"How does he keep doing that?" Phoebe looked a little scared as she grasped Charlie's arm.

"I've known you all a very long time." He pulled a tiny gold book from his pocket. It looked so small against his hands that Charlie felt sure it was from a doll's house. They watched, speechless, as Professor Brittle opened the book, placed his glasses on his nose and began to read. "Bella Bronson. Born July 14th, parents John and Mandy, only child." He turned a page in the book, and it seemed to grow larger suddenly. "Zoe Decker. Born February 22nd, lives with her dad Michael and three older brothers." The book grew yet again as he turned another page. "Daniel Foster." On and on he read, and each time he turned a page the book grew bigger and bigger until finally it was the size of an old-fashioned encyclopaedia and he had to hold it in both hands. "And last but by no means least, Charlie Woods."

A chiming sound from inside Professor Brittle's pocket made him slam the book shut. It instantly returned to its tiny state where it was immediately placed back in the coat pocket from whence it came.

"How does he do it?" Zoe whispered to Becky as Professor Brittle busied himself with the golden list. He seemed to be checking off the names in his head, reading each one, looking up, nodding and then reading the next.

"Where's Chelsea?" he said suddenly. "Chelsea Hicks? Anyone seen Chelsea Hicks?"

"Please, sir," Alide spoke up. "Chelsea didn't come to this school." Charlie knew from primary school that Chelsea and Alide were best friends.

"What do you mean she didn't come to this school?" Professor Brittle re-read his list and then pulled the tiny book out again. "I just read out her details to you all."

"I did think that was a little strange," Alide commented. "But I just thought it was because it was so last minute her not coming here."

"Well, where did she go?" Professor Brittle placed the book away again and made the paper disappear with a click of his fingers.

"They had to move away," Alide said, looking close to tears that her best friend was no longer around. "She's at St. Agatha's in Cornwall."

"Well, that's fantastic news." This seemed to please Professor Brittle immensely, but Alide was now sobbing her heart out. "No need to cry, Alide."

"But, sir," Becky said, placing a comforting arm around Alide, "they're best friends."

"I can see that, Becky." He took his glasses off and tucked them back onto his waistcoat. "Still no need to cry."

"But she's hundreds of miles away, sir," Becky explained. "Alide and Chelsea have been friends since nursery school. They thought they were going to high school together."

"And so they are."

The children looked at each other and then looked at Professor Brittle.

"Sir?" Charlie piped up. "How can they be? Alide's here and Chelsea's down south."

"But she's not," Professor Brittle stated to raised eyebrows and questioning looks from the children. "She's right here at Brittle's Academy, just like you."

CHAPTER 4

"Well, as my nan says, that's about as clear as mud." Daniel exchanged confused glances with the others.

"Has anyone got an older brother or sister at this school?" Bella asked, receiving nods of agreement or shaking of heads. "Have they ever mentioned a Professor Brittle or Brittle's Academy?"

"My brother Alex came here a few years ago," Charlie piped in. "He never mentioned it."

"Not one of my brother's talked about it either," Zoe agreed. "I'm sure I'd have remembered a name like Brittle."

"Perhaps he's not a real teacher," Daniel remarked. "He could be an alien coming to take us to another planet." He wriggled his fingers at Becky and Alide as if they were tentacles, and they squealed.

"Of course he's a real teacher," Sandeep scolded. "He wouldn't be allowed in here if he wasn't."

"Exactly," Bella said. "Mrs Martell knew exactly who he was. In fact, if you'd all been listening, he said he has a class list every year."

"All right, smarty pants," Daniel teased. "We don't all hang on every word the teacher says."

"I do not!" Bella huffed her shoulders up. "I just happen to think it's very important to listen when the teachers are talking, that's all."

"Isn't that what I just said?" He looked at Charlie, who shrugged.

"Where's he gone?" Martin asked, looking over his shoulder and around the room. "He's vanished."

"How can he have vanished?"

"Well do you see him?"

"He can't just leave us."

"Looks like he has."

"I'm still here." The professor's voice boomed out as if he was all around the room.

"I don't like this anymore," Alide said. She and Becky were huddling together, a look of fright on their faces.

"There's something not right about the whole thing." Bella stood up. "I'm going to find Mrs Martell and tell her what's going on."

"But then you'll miss out on all the fun." The gold cloud that had heralded Professor Brittle's arrival returned, but instead of turning into a person, it just hovered in front of them all.

"Maybe I want to miss out on the fun," Bella said directly to the cloud. "Maybe I just want to come to school, learn from my teachers and pass my exams at the end of it all so I can do my A levels and get into Cambridge."

A few of the boys sniggered at this, and she turned and glared at them.

"There's nothing wrong with dreams and aspirations, boys." The cloud moved in front of them and turned a darker colour. "I won't have anyone belittling another pupil at my school."

"Yes, sir."

"Sorry, sir."

The cloud lightened again and moved off towards the back of the theatre and stopped in front of the door they had all come through earlier.

"Are you coming or not?" the cloud said. After a hesitant pause, the children stood up and walked down the middle, following the path the cloud had taken. "Bella?" The others hadn't noticed Bella still standing near the stage, her hands folded in indignation.

"I'm not coming."

The cloud floated back towards her. "Why not?"

"Because I want to go to a real school, with real teachers that don't turn into clouds or have tiny little books in their pockets with the details about all their students." She talked to the cloud as if it was a person.

"I'll do you a deal, Bella." Professor Brittle's face appeared at the front of the cloud. "Come with us now, spend the day, and if you really don't like the school, I will personally re-enrol you here at Park Hill."

"Re-enrol?" These were clearly the only words Bella had picked up on. "Re-enrol?" she repeated, pulling out her mobile phone, which Charlie noticed was the latest iPhone. "My mother shall be hearing about this." She looked into the phone and it lit up. "Okay, Siri, call Mum."

"Perhaps re-enrol wasn't the right word." A hand reached out of the cloud and scooped the phone from her hand. "Just come and see." Professor Brittle's voice was soft, the cloud hand resting on her shoulder.

"Come on, Bella."

"Yes, come on, Bella."

"What have you got to lose?"

"Well my mother is one of the governors here and I can assure you right now that she will be having very strong words with Mrs Martell and you'll be out of a job quicker than..." Her words trailed off mid-sentence. "What are you all staring at?"

Bella folded her arms across her chest and looked back at the others who were all now standing stock still, their mouths wide open in shock and surprise.

"How is she doing it?" Alide whispered to Becky.

"This day is just getting crazier and crazier," Charlie said. Martin, Sandeep and Daniel nodded in agreement.

"Will you tell me what you are all staring at?" Bella shouted. "Ow!" She rubbed her head. "This really isn't a laughing matter."

Phoebe tried hard to stifle a giggle.

"Ouch!" Bella rubbed her head again. "What on earth keeps hitting me?" This time she looked up only to find herself six feet off the ground, her head touching the ceiling. "Aaargh!" Bella looked at her feet, realised she was floating, panicked and shot straight down to the ground, landing in a heap on the floor.

"Are you okay?" The gold cloud re-formed into Professor Brittle who helped Bella stand. "You're stronger than I thought."

"Stronger?" Bella rubbed her elbows and knees.

"Professor Brittle?" Charlie tugged on his coat, trying to get his attention. "Sir?"

"Yes, Charlie?" Professor Brittle turned to face him, a now limping Bella in the crook of his arm.

"There's someone watching through the door, sir."

Professor Brittle followed the direction that Charlie was pointing. "I don't see anyone, Charlie." He helped Bella to join the others, Charlie walking behind.

"Honestly, sir." Charlie looked back towards the door. "There, look, right there."

"There's no one there." Teddy looked to the door, as did the others.

"Stop winding us up, Charlie," Alide scolded. "We're all on edge as it is, what with teachers appearing from gold clouds and now Bella floating in mid-air. We don't need…" She froze. "Ghost!"

CHAPTER 5

The girls screamed, as did a few of the boys, as a pale-faced lady waved at them all through the glass door.

"That's not a ghost." Professor Brittle made sure Bella was sitting down on one of the benches before opening the door. "This is Professor Peculiar."

"Pleased to meet you all." The group of children stared open-mouthed at the new arrival. She was dressed in a blue and white striped suit. Pale blonde, almost white, hair lay neatly around her shoulders. She wore a matching blue hat with white lace that sat slightly backwards on her head so you couldn't actually see the top of it, just the wide brim that elegantly shielded her face.

"Is something amiss, Percy?" Professor Brittle asked as the new arrival's hat appeared to be wriggling.

"No, no, everything's fine." She pulled out a long thin piece of ebony from her sleeve and tapped her hat gently. The piece of hardwood glowed blue for just a split second and the hat went immediately still. "We were just wondering when you'd be joining us." She slipped the ebony into her sleeve. "The rest of the first years are all waiting for you and the other children have gone back to their schools now they have their timetables."

Charlie's head hurt from all the information it was trying to gather, his mind whirling from all the new things he'd seen. When he looked at the other children, their faces held the same confusion.

"Well then," Professor Brittle said as he helped Bella back onto her feet, "we'd best be off."

Professor Peculiar moved to one side to allow Professor Brittle and Bella by. "Off you go." She ushered the rest of the children after Professor Brittle before following behind, adjusting her hat as she went.

They walked in silence along the corridor of Park Hill Secondary, passing many classrooms already filled with pupils and teachers. Up the stairs to the second floor, and then the third—a slightly harder task to do with the still limping Bella.

"Where are we going?" Sandeep asked Charlie as they walked past what appeared to be science laboratories. "Is he our science teacher or something?"

"Weren't you listening to anything?" Teddy called over his shoulder. "We're going to a different school and he's the head of it."

"But how can we be going to a different school?" Sandeep looked at Charlie who shrugged his shoulders.

"Here we are then." They had reached the end of the corridor and were now staring at a blank wall. "All ready?"

"Er…" Phoebe began. "Ready for what, sir?"

"To see Brittle's Academy, of course," Professor Brittle said, beaming from ear to ear. "Surely I explained that to you?" The blank expressions on their faces gave him his answer. "No? Oh well, we're nearly there so I won't bother with that now." He tried to reach one hand into his coat pocket, then, switching Bella into his other arm, tried with his other hand. "Professor Peculiar, could you do the honours please? I'm a little tied up, shall we say."

"It would be my pleasure, Professor."

The children moved aside to allow Professor Peculiar to walk past them, each letting out a gasp of surprise as she passed them by.

"Is that…" Alide who was near the front of the group stared in disbelief. "…a cat?"

Where most hats had ribbons or flowers, sometimes even fruit, this hat was different. Curled up with the tip of its tail tucked under its nose was a bluey grey Siamese cat. Not a little plastic one, or even a little furry one; this was a life-size cat with pointy ears and long whiskers, and it appeared to be sleeping.

"Of course it's a cat," Professor Peculiar said. "It's not a dog. Whoever heard of a dog on a hat? That would just be absurd." She tutted and pulled out the long piece of ebony once again. The children instinctively moved forwards to see.

Professor Peculiar waved the piece of ebony, that could only be described as a wand, in a large rectangular shape over the bare white wall of the school. As she did this, the wand glowed blue at one end and, after nodding her head in satisfaction, she placed it once more in her sleeve.

"Just a few more seconds," Professor Brittle said. "I can hear it coming." The children all looked at each other, straining their ears.

"Can you hear anything?" Teddy whispered. "I can't hear anything."

"Sush!" Charlie said, placing his finger on his lips. "I can. It sounds like an elevator."

"Don't be so—" Teddy was cut off mid-sentence as two silver doors suddenly appeared in the wall with a button to the side showing an arrow pointing upwards.

With a loud ping, the doors slid open to reveal a completely normal looking elevator. It was so unbelievably normal that Charlie found himself giggling.

"Anything the matter, Charlie?" Professor Brittle asked as he and Professor Peculiar helped Bella inside.

"It's just … well, I was sort of…" Charlie didn't really know how to explain. "What with everything else that's been going on, I kind of expected something a little more interesting."

"It's just an elevator, Charlie." Professor Brittle ushered them all inside and pressed the one and only button on the elevator's panel. "They're really not the most interesting of things. They just serve a purpose, that's all."

The doors slid shut, and the elevator lurched slightly as the brakes released and up it went and went and went.

"I feel sick." Phoebe placed her hand to her mouth. "I don't like lifts, or heights. How much further?"

"Nearly there." Professor Peculiar placed a comforting hand on her shoulder just as the elevator lurched to a stop and pinged again to announce its arrival.

The doors slid open, and the children immediately shielded their eyes from the sunlight that blinded them.

"Welcome to Brittle's Academy for the Magically Unstable." Bella, whose leg seemed to have magically healed itself, stepped out first.

"Oh my life!" she said, turning around to talk to the others. "We're in the clouds."

CHAPTER 6

"Don't be so silly, Bella," Alide said as she stepped out. "Argh!" She stepped back again, clinging onto the elevator doors as if her life depended on it.

"You're not going to fall through, you know." Professor Peculiar moved to the front of the elevator and took hold of Bella's hand. After a few steps, she turned back. "See, nothing to worry about."

All the others, except for Charlie and Alide, barged out together and started laughing and joking around. "Come on, Alide," Charlie said, looking out at the others who were apparently standing on clouds. Thick white fluffy clouds. "If they can do it, so can we." He offered her his arm. "Here, hold onto me and we'll go together."

Alide grabbed Charlie's arm with a scared smile.

"One, two, three." And they both took a huge step out from the elevator, their feet landing on what felt like hard rock.

"The clouds are especially thick today," Professor Brittle said, slapping Charlie gently on the shoulder. "Normally you can see everything perfectly, but now and again, and especially if it's raining, well … if it's raining, even I sometimes have trouble believing it's actually there."

"Believing what's where, sir?" Alide asked, still scared to move further in case this unseen floor suddenly disappeared.

"Why, the academy, of course." He pulled out a beautiful dark brown wand, like Professor Peculiar's but slightly thicker, and when he swished it around, it glowed gold.

The clouds seemed to part instantly revealing a wide stone path that led right from the elevator and out into the sky. As the three of them walked, the clouds moved to allow them to see their feet but would return the moment they had stepped away.

"Are we really in the sky?" Charlie heard Bella ask Professor Peculiar, who nodded and did a similar thing with her wand. For a split second, the clouds evaporated completely, and they all found themselves peering down at the world below.

Charlie could see the town so perfectly. Park Hill with its grey stone buildings and huge cross-country fields was surrounded by the many different sized houses. People and cars were going about their daily business, and there, clearly seen on the corner, was the shop Charlie would often go to in the morning when they'd run out of milk.

"We're only a few hundred metres up," Professor Brittle explained.

"But can't everyone down there see this?" Charlie asked, certain he would have noticed a large stone path floating in mid-air above him.

"No, the NUMS don't have a clue," he said, and then suddenly sped off as he realised Professor Peculiar had stopped.

"NUMS?" Charlie looked at Alide, who looked back, equally blank.

"I don't like this, Charlie." She still held tight to his arm. "I don't like it one little bit. I want to go back down to Park Hill where the floor is the floor and people and things don't appear out of thin air."

"I know what you mean, Alide." He squeezed her arm. "But aren't you just a little bit excited?"

She shook her head.

"Not even a little?"

"Well, maybe just a little." She laughed slightly. "But I think I'm still more scared than excited."

They looked ahead at a clinking and clanging sound. The professors and the rest of the children had reached the biggest pair of black gates Charlie had ever seen. They must have been at least ten feet high and ten feet wide with smooth spikes on the top. They were currently opening inwards and their movement caused the clouds to swirl around, revealing huge stone walls as far as the eye could see on both sides.

Everyone else had moved inside the gates, but Charlie and Alide still had a few steps to go.

"Come on, you two," Sandeep shouted. "It's amazing."

Whether it was the look of excitement on Sandeep's face or just that they wanted to get off the floating path, Alide and Charlie started to run.

"Wow!" Charlie slowed just inside the gates, taking in the scene around him. They were in a courtyard, a long, stone-paved courtyard that stretched the entire length of an enormous house. Because of its sheer size, it reminded Charlie slightly of Buckingham Palace, but as he had never actually visited London, he wasn't sure which was bigger, but he had the feeling it was this place.

Row upon row of windows stood in perfectly symmetrical columns, and Charlie counted six floors in total, and another window nestled into the apex roof that stood at the very top of the house, directly above the door. The door, which currently stood wide open, had a sign arched above which read Brittle's Academy and had been chiselled into the stone of the building.

"We'd best take the shortcut." Professor Brittle gathered everyone closely around him. "We're already very late and it really doesn't do for the

Headmaster to be late. Besides, there will be plenty of time for exploring later." And with these words, he swirled his wand around and around in a huge circle until all of them were encased in gold smoke.

"I don't like this." Alide found Charlie's hand and squeezed it tightly.

The outside of the house whirled before them as it appeared to be spinning, or was it them who were spinning? Charlie didn't really know. All he did know was that he was starting to feel slightly sick at the motion and closed his eyes tightly, hoping it would help.

The spinning stopped as quickly as it had started.

Tentatively, Charlie opened one eye and then the other, his mouth opening as wide as his eyes were now at what stood before him.

CHAPTER 7

Professor Brittle and Professor Peculiar disappeared, leaving the small group of children from Park Hill in what could only be described as a giant library. Row upon row of books stood upon huge shelves that reached from floor to ceiling and wall to wall.

Huge arched doors stood at either end, and the occasional smaller door could be seen amongst the book shelves. Upon closer inspection, Charlie could even see doors higher up in the rows. He wondered why on earth there would be doors when there were clearly no floors behind them, and a drop of a considerable height from one at the top, which he was guessing to be as high as the whole house.

But apart from all the books, it was the sheer amount of noise and people that astounded Charlie. All along the floor were groups of children standing and chatting. The groups varied in size from five or six to over thirty, but each group had children the same age as they were.

Their appearance in the library hadn't caused so much as a stir from the other children, and Charlie wondered if strange things like this had been happening all morning. After all, hadn't Professor Brittle said they were late?

All the children in each group were dressed the same, and it was obvious to Charlie that, like them, they had come from different schools. There were black blazers, blue blazers and grey blazers. Red ties, yellow ties, plain ties and striped ties, but standing at the top end of the room on a wooden stage were twelve pupils dressed completely differently. They were a few years older, about fifteen, Charlie would have said, and dressed in the uniform he had seen the boy and girl wearing that had entered Park Hill earlier through the other entrance.

Whereas most of the children wore the standard school blazer that reached just to the top of your legs, this blazer was longer and was different for the boys and girls. The boys wore more of a frock coat, like Charlie's uncle had worn at his wedding last year, but this one had a slightly raised, rounded collar and dark beading that made it look almost military in style. Crisp white shirts with the same rounded collar were worn underneath and black trousers covered shiny black shoes.

There were six different colours. One boy and one girl in each colour. Emerald green, cobalt blue, darkest red, chocolate brown, deep purple, and gold.

The girls were dressed in a slightly different style. Although they still wore black trousers, these were tucked into chunky black knee-high boots that reminded Charlie a little of biker's boots. Their blazers, like the boys', reached just below their knees but were pulled in at the waist and buttoned up to the collar where just the top of a white shirt could be seen. Again, there was dark beading, giving them a military appearance.

"Can we all be quiet please?" Professor Brittle's voice seemed to boom all around the room, and everyone went deathly silent, turning towards the stage at the front.

Alide was still holding tight to Charlie's hand, her face pale and scared.

Charlie hadn't noticed before, but as well as the twelve pupils, he also saw a number of strangely dressed adults who he presumed were the teachers, one of them Professor Peculiar, who was standing next to the boy and girl dressed in blue. In fact, all the pairs now had an adult standing next to them— except for the ones in gold who were still standing on their own.

There were a number of other adults present on the stage as well. Like the children, they were in groups, and Charlie wondered who on earth they all were.

"Can this day get any stranger?" he whispered to Alide, and immediately regretted it as she choked back a little sob.

"Welcome everyone." It was Professor Brittle again, and although Charlie could hear him loud and clear, he couldn't actually see him. "I know it's been a very confusing morning for you with mysterious going ons and all sorts of weird and wonderful things to take in, but this is just the beginning of a brand-new adventure for you all. By the end of today you will all know more about our wonderful academy, but for some of you, it will be your last."

There was an audible gasp from around the room.

"Maybe used the wrong words there," Professor Brittle continued. "What I meant to say was that although all of you are here today because you have shown promise, not all of you will continue on your journey here at Brittle's, and this is what your first day here is all about. You need to get to know us, and we need to get to know you."

There was a collective sigh as the children visibly relaxed.

"Can we go home, Charlie?" Alide asked. "I want to go home. I don't like it here."

Charlie could feel her trembling beside him and did his best to comfort her. "It'll be alright," he soothed. "We're all together, and there's lots of other children here as well."

She looked suspiciously around the room, then suddenly gasped. "Chelsea!" she screamed at the top of her voice and, after dropping Charlie's hand, ran as quickly as she could, barging through the groups of children who were staring at her.

"Alide?" Charlie recognised Chelsea immediately.

"Miss Valberga?" A stern voice and a brown cloud appeared, and just as she was about to reach Chelsea, Alide stopped dead in her tracks.

"I can't move my feet," Alide mouthed back to Charlie.

A brown cloud swirled and, as the gold one had changed into Professor Brittle, this one changed into a rather squat-looking man with a bald head. He wore a long brown coat, brown trousers and a brown shirt. In fact, everything about him was brown, including his eyes which were too close together, and he had a nose too large for his face.

"We do not tolerate behaviour like that at Brittle's Academy, Miss Valberga." He swished his wand and Alide found herself skidding backwards towards the Park Hill group of children. "Kindly refrain from such an outburst again."

Alide blushed red as the entire hall laughed, staring at her. The Park Hill children instinctively formed a protective circle around her.

Professor Brittle's voice returned. "Yes, well, thank you, Professor Bones. I'm sure she won't do it again. And enough of the interruptions. It's time for a little break and then we'll all meet outside in the gardens for some practise. Now, make sure you all get something to eat and drink. You're going to need the energy. Don't want any accidents now, do we?" He laughed. When no one else joined in, he realised his mistake. "Sorry, shouldn't have said that."

"You heard the Headmaster," Professor Bones said, staring at them with folded arms. The other groups of children had started to move out of the door behind the stage. "Don't want any accidents." And with this, he laughed and disappeared into his brown cloud.

CHAPTER 8

The gardens of the academy were as large and impressive as the house. White trestle tables stood laden with various foods and drinks. Just like with the lift, Charlie was surprised to see a very ordinary fayre spread before them.

Sandwiches cut into triangles were stuffed with cheese, ham, salad or chicken. Mini sausages, pork pies, rice dishes, pasta salad and a number of fruits were placed neatly alongside a variety of different coloured drinks ranging from plain old water to fruit juices, and something bright blue that Charlie wasn't really sure about. It bubbled slightly in its plastic cup, and tiny wisps of blue smoke came out of it every time one of the little bubbles burst.

"I'm not touching that." Bella was first from their little group to reach the tables and grabbed a cup of water, two sandwiches and an apple.

"Nor me." Sandeep took orange juice, a huge spoonful of vegetable rice, and balanced a banana on his head. In fact, not one of the Park Hill group even looked twice at the smoking liquid until Alide came along.

"Can you believe Chelsea is here?" Alide said. The change in her was immense. She was more like the old Alide that Charlie knew from primary school, smiling and happy and almost skipping with glee. "Ooohh! Raspberryade, my favourite." She picked up one of the cups and downed it in seconds while the others stared at her in disbelief.

"Alide!" Phoebe warned. "I don't think that was raspberryade."

"Tasted like it." She hiccupped a little. "Beg pardon."

"Hurry up, first years, we haven't got all day." Professor Bones had reappeared along with the boy and girl dressed in brown. "Gather around please." He clapped his hands for attention. "Now then, in the grounds is a tall oak tree. It's been here for hundreds of years. All we want you to do is climb to the top of it." And with this, he and the pair of students vanished into thin air.

"Climb a tree?" Teddy was already running with the rest of the children before Charlie even had time to finish his sausage roll.

He ambled after the others, down the long lawn of green grass surrounded by a dense forest of thick trees. By the time he reached the oak tree there were already at least fifty pupils halfway up its branches, and hundreds more trying to find the best starting point.

"You not having a go, Charlie?" Phoebe asked as she threw her blazer onto the ground and rolled up her sleeves.

"Nah." He started peeling the orange he'd brought down with him. "My mum would kill me if I damaged this uniform." He sat on the slight hill, pulled off his shoes and rubbed his pinched toes in relief.

Before long, a few other children had joined him, and they sat in companionable silence watching as grey blazers, blue blazers and black blazers blurred up the tree.

"I knew this would be too much for you, Mr Woods." Professor Bones appeared behind him. "Scared you might fall and break something?"

"Not at all, sir." He threw a segment of orange into his mouth and squinted up at him. "Just a bit hot for climbing trees, that's all."

"Well!" Professor Bones seemed to stretch his shoulders up to make him seem taller. "Of all the insolent, rude and—"

"Professor, look!" The older girl dressed in brown caught his attention. "The first one." Charlie looked to the top of the tree, where Teddy Johnson was frantically waving and cheering.

"Thankfully, Mr Woods, some pupils are a little braver than you." And with a swish of his wand, Teddy disappeared. "The House of Oak doesn't take cowards." And with this, he stormed away, his brown coat blowing out behind him.

"Blimey, you're brave." A red-haired boy who was sitting next to him remarked.

"You haven't met my mum," Charlie replied. "She's already warned me not to damage my clothes in any way, and trust me, I'm more scared of her than him."

An hour later, Professor Bones called a halt to proceedings. There had definitely been more failures than successes, and quite a few walking wounded were rubbing ankles or dabbing cuts.

The Park Hill group re-joined Charlie, but though Chelsea had now joined them, they were still three short.

"Where's Teddy, Sandeep and Bella?" Phoebe asked, nursing a nasty looking cut on her elbow.

"I don't know." Becky looked around. "But I'm sure there's a few missing from the other groups as well.

"Michael and Jayne are missing from St. Agatha's," Chelsea said.

When Charlie looked around, he was positive the rather large group of children that had been in the library this morning was slightly smaller.

"The House of Oak thanks you for your participation today." It was the boy dressed in brown that spoke. "Unfortunately, only a few of you have proved worthy enough to join our ranks. We wish you well on your further quests and bid you good day."

He bowed deeply, then, with a slight sneer on his face, followed Professor Bones and the girl back into the school.

"What was all that about?" Alide asked, confused. "House of Oak?"

"The House of Violet welcomes you." There was no time to answer as in a puff of purple smoke another teacher appeared, again with two older pupils. "My prefects and I would like you to accompany us to the first floor."

Charlie groaned as he replaced his shoes and stood up.

"Well, at least we know those older ones are prefects now." Chelsea linked arms with Alide. "I think it's your school house, you know, like in primary school when we were in Manor."

"Yeah, but in primary we were just told what house we were in. We weren't given a load of tests to do." Daniel trudged along with the others, following the female teacher who was dressed in a long flowing robe of pale purple with a hood and long sleeves.

They found themselves standing in front of a huge wooden staircase that reached right up to the top floor. It curved elegantly around the walls, and Charlie felt dizzy when he looked up.

"Now then, children," the teacher said, clapping her hands, "I am Mrs White." There were a few giggles. "Is there something funny with my name?" There was silence. "No? The fact that I'm wearing purple but called White? No? That's not funny?" She looked sternly at them all, and Charlie noticed with a start that even her eyes were purple, not deep purple but a sort of lavender colour. "So now we've cleared that up." She drew her hands together and smiled. "Just up there on the first floor, you will find a pair of double doors. All you have to do is open them and get to the other side of the room." And just as Professor Bones had done, she vanished.

"Climbing trees and opening doors." Martin laughed. "These tasks are easy."

They soon realised, however, that although opening the door was easy, getting to the other side was impossible because after everyone had stepped into the room, the floor started to drop away, leaving every single one of them balancing on a tiny stone pillar.

CHAPTER 9

Some of the girls screamed, some of the boys screamed, some stood as still as statues, scared to move even an inch whilst others, who were nearer the edges, were already trying to find ways of getting to the thin ledges that had been left when the floor dropped away.

"Are they trying to kill us?" said the red-haired boy who'd spoken to Charlie as they sat watching the tree-climbing test. Everyone was about a metre away from everyone else, just a little out of jumping reach. Not that you could jump anywhere anyway because every single pillar had a pupil standing on it, so unless you intended shoving someone else off, you were stuck.

"Martin?" Charlie saw the look of intent in his eyes. Only one pillar stood between Martin and the platform on the other side. On this platform was a rather small, timid, blonde-haired girl in a purple blazer, grey skirt and grey knee-high socks. "You can't do that, Martin." Charlie could see he was trying to judge how much force he needed to put in his jump.

"It's the only way, Charlie," he said, and took a giant leap from his pillar, into the air and puff. He disappeared into what Charlie could only describe as a black hole. Everyone on their pillars who witnessed this event pulled their feet closer together and made themselves even smaller.

"What's that noise?" a tall, gangly boy near to the doors they first came through called out. "It's getting louder. Listen."

"It's coming from underneath us." Charlie strained his ears and stared into the black chasm below.

"It sounds like wings," a couple of the girls said in unison.

"Birds?"

"Bats?"

"Oh my word, look!" Becky said, and pointed as the unmistakable sound of a huge pair of wings flapping slowly and gently became louder and louder. Silvery white tips emerged first, followed immediately, and shooting straight upwards into the room, by a gleaming white horse with a long silver mane and tail. It spun around the room, swooping and darting with a speed and grace that defied its sheer size.

Within seconds another appeared, and another, until there were over thirty of the beautiful creatures gliding elegantly around the room.

"Are we meant to catch them, do you think?" Becky asked.

"With what?" Chelsea replied. "Ties and shoelaces?"

Charlie watched the horses; they seemed to be searching for something, hovering just slightly above each student before moving onto the next. Suddenly, one of them descended gently down and nuzzled the little girl Martin had been staring at.

She reached her fingers out and stroked its smooth nose, giggling as it blew gently on her hand. The horse bowed its head, almost motionless, just the slight beating of its wings to stop it from sinking any lower.

"I think he wants you to get on," Charlie urged the little girl, who was now looking ever so slightly nervous. As if in agreement, the horse whinnied, grab the girl's skirt and threw her onto his back, his wings beating faster and faster to move him away from the pillar and onto the platform. The little girl immediately vanished in a puff of purple smoke.

The horses started taking on other passengers, some came willingly, climbing onto their backs and screaming in delight as they flew up into the air, while others, like the little girl, needed a little more persuading, but each one disappeared as she had done as soon as they reached the platform. The horse would then return to collect another child.

It was then Charlie noticed one of the horses was still circling around. It was even bigger than the others and its mane and tail were purple not silver. At almost the same time that Charlie looked up, it looked down and swooped towards him so fast that Charlie could feel the wind from its wings.

It stood in front of him, its huge brown eyes looking into his own. Charlie felt lost for a second. The world swam before him, a beautiful haze of purple mist that seemed to cloud his mind, and he felt a peacefulness he had never felt before.

"Charlie!" Alide's screaming brought him back into consciousness. The horse had bent its head ready for Charlie to climb on his back. "Charlie!" Alide's tone made him turn. Somehow, she'd slipped and was clinging onto the edge of her stone pillar for dear life. He was the nearest to her. The horse whinnied, urging him to climb aboard, but his friend mattered more.

With a brief look up to the heavens, he leapt onto a pillar and then the next. Luckily most of them were empty now as the children who hadn't been picked up by the horses had summoned up the courage to jump over the now empty pillars.

"Hang on, Alide, I'm nearly there." Just one more pillar and he'd be with her, but what was he going to do when he actually reached her? There wasn't enough room for two. Before he had time to think, the purple-maned horse swooped past, scooping Alide up onto its back and flying her safely to the platform. Unlike the others, though, there was no smoke, and she remained firmly where she was until Chelsea reached her, followed swiftly by Charlie.

"A wonderful display, children," Mrs White said. She and the two prefects re-appeared, throwing sugar lumps to the horses. "Only the purest of heart can ride the winged horses."

"Please, Miss?" Charlie asked. "What happened to Martin?"

"Mr Woods, always thinking of others." She smiled at him. "The House of Violet would be honoured to have you, but alas, another claims you as its own."

"But, Miss, where's Martin?" It was Alide's turn to ask.

"The selfish of heart have no place in the House of Violet, or indeed in the academy." The two prefects spoke this time. "His time here is over and oblivion will claim him."

"Oblivion?" Chelsea squeaked. "That doesn't sound very good."

"It is the worst kind of hell imaginable." And with this statement, Mrs White and the two prefects turned into purple smoke and swirled away through the now open door.

CHAPTER 10

"Well, don't we all look a sorry sight?" A lady was standing on the other side of the doors. Although she was dressed in black, she seemed to glow red. Not an angry red but a soothing, soft red that instantly eased Charlie's fears about Martin. "Let's get you all upstairs and looked after, shall we?" She seemed to float as she walked, her long dress hardly moving, and the bewildered group of children, now even smaller in size, followed without hesitation or delay.

"I'm not going in anymore rooms or doing any more tests," Alide said to Charlie as she took his hand and Chelsea's. "Teddy, Sandeep and Bella all disappeared after climbing that tree. Zoe flew off on a horse into a puff of purple smoke, and Martin has been sent to oblivion."

"I'm sure he won't come to any harm." Charlie wasn't sure about this at all but didn't think Alide was the best person to discuss it with.

"Here we are now." The second floor, like the first, was a myriad of doors. The staircase continued weaving its way around further up, but the lady stopped in front of a room which smelt of flowers. "In you all go." Some needed more encouragement than others after the last room they had entered with its falling floor, but as they watched others going in with no adverse effects, it wasn't long until the entire group was inside.

The room seemed to hug them as they entered. To Charlie it felt like Christmas Eve when he'd been little. He would wrap himself up in a blanket with a mug of hot chocolate and stare out of his window hoping to catch sight of Santa's sleigh.

Most of the pupils had fallen into the array of soft chairs and cushions that were scattered around, but a few, including Edward and Becky, were moving around the room, handing out drinks and biscuits they'd found laid out on a beautifully carved wooden table. Charlie noticed a cupboard in one corner, its door wide open with a pile of red blankets stacked neatly inside.

Remembering that people in shock often started shaking, he grabbed a few of them and started offering them around the room. Alide and Chelsea smiled gratefully and huddled together under the same one, chatting and sipping what Charlie thought looked like Chamomile tea.

"I feel so much better now," he heard one girl say as she sighed contentedly.

"It's just so relaxing in here," another replied.

"Can't we stay for the rest of the day?" a blonde boy with spikey hair asked.

"I'm afraid not, my dears," the lady who still hadn't introduced herself replied. "The House of Sage awaits you."

"But I don't want to do any more tests," Becky said, finally sipping her own cup of tea.

"Oh, my dear, you don't have to." The lady took out a long black wand.

"You just said…" Becky and many of the others were confused.

"Yes, the House of Sage awaits, but not for you." Her wand started to glow red. "I am Doctor Payne, head of the House of Camellia, and all of you who selflessly helped others while you yourself were in need are just the people we are looking for." Her wand shot beams of red light around the room, and children jumped as students vanished once more in front of their eyes.

Charlie closed his eyes, waiting for the red light to fall on him, but when he heard chairs scraping and shoes shuffling, he opened one eye, quickly followed by another, and found Alide and Chelsea standing in front of him, staring at him oddly.

"You okay, Charlie?" Chelsea looked concerned.

"Well, I was kind of expecting to…" He didn't know what he was expecting, really. "…you know, get beamed up with the others."

Doctor Payne had left, leaving a few lost-looking faces around.

"Perhaps you did it wrong?" Alide suggested. "You were the only one handing out blankets whereas the others were giving out that tea and those delicious biscuits."

"You could be right." He looked around for the rest of the Park Hill group. "Only seven of us left now."

"Seven?" Alide scanned the room nervously.

"Well, eight if you count Chelsea. The House of Camellia claimed three of us." He double checked in his head. "Just you, me, Phoebe, Tasha, Daniel and those other two boys who must have come from a different primary school." As he spoke, those two individuals joined them.

"We went to Manor Brooke Primary," one of the boys said. "I'm Will and this here is Dom." They all nodded their heads in welcome and introduced themselves. "It's a weird place here and no mistake."

Everyone agreed with him.

"You mean six." The group looked at Tasha. "There's six of us."

"What do you mean six?" Charlie looked at the little group and was just about to count again when a blue-grey cat slinked into the room and started staring at them all.

"Is that…?" Daniel looked at the cat and then at Charlie who nodded.

"It's the cat off Professor Peculiar's hat." Charlie was sure of it. "But what's it doing here?"

"Perhaps Professor Peculiar is the head of Sage?" Dom suggested, but for some reason Charlie didn't think this was true.

"Percy!" It was Professor Peculiar. "Persephone Peculiar the fourth!" She entered the room and seemed somewhat unbalanced in her walk. She was tripping over and falling to one side. "Get back here immediately. I don't know how many times I have to tell you not to wander off." She was clearly talking to the cat who was paying absolutely no attention to her and was now busy licking her paws and washing behind her ears. "Just because I took my attention off you to gather my students, you think you can run off and do what you like. Well, my girl, you can't." And with a swish of her wand and a shot of blue light the cat meowed and flew through the air, landing on the Professor's hat with a thump.

With an authoritative air, the Professor readjusted her skirt and jacket, tilted her hat a little and walked elegantly back out of the room.

"What was all that about?" Will asked.

"No idea." Charlie replied. "But what I'm more worried about is where Alide and Chelsea have gone."

CHAPTER 11

"It's not just Alide and Chelsea," Tasha said. "Look around."

Charlie scanned the room and was rather shocked to discover how very small the group of children left had become. From the hundreds and hundreds gathered in the library that morning there were now maybe a little over two hundred left.

"Where's everyone gone?" Will asked. "I saw the ones evaporate ... is evaporate the right word?" he asked himself. "Well, I shall use it anyway. They went off with Doctor Payne, but we've lost way more than that."

"They must have joined Professor Peculiar's house." Daniel looked towards the door where the other children seemed to be gathering.

"But how?" Charlie asked. "There wasn't a test."

They had no time for further discussion as standing by the doors was the most beautiful lady Charlie had ever seen. She had deep chestnut hair that peeked out from the dark green cowl wrapped around her head. She was accompanied by her two prefects, and Charlie knew this was the head of Sage.

"Good afternoon, children." Her voice had a slight Irish accent and Charlie found himself hanging on her every word. "Now you've all had lunch, it's time to get those brains of yours working. Follow me upstairs."

"Lunch?" Dom asked. "I've only had one of them biscuit things. Don't tell me that was lunch?"

The prefects heard him. "One of Doctor Payne's specialities. A full three-course meal in a tiny biscuit. Perfect when you're short of time or off on your travels."

The two prefects walked with the remaining Park Hill students. This was the first time any of them had done this and Charlie took the opportunity to ask some questions.

"Where did my other friends go?"

The girl prefect looked quizzically at him.

"They were here after the Camellia test but vanished when Professor Peculiar appeared."

"Honestly." The two prefects laughed. "Just because she's psychic, she assumes everyone else is and forgets to tell anyone what she's doing and why she's doing it."

"Psychic?" Charlie asked.

"The House of Borage," the boy prefect explained. "The happiest, most positive of all the houses."

"Can be a little vain." The girl explained, to which the boy agreed.

The girl nodded. "Yes, they're always doing something a little different with their uniform so they stand out more. And they're psychic."

The girl could see Charlie still had questions. "You remember the blue drink when you first arrived? Well, to most of us it was bubbling and smoking away." Charlie nodded. "That was a spell. To anyone who belongs in the House of Borage, they would see straight through it and be drawn to it immediately."

"Alide drank it," Charlie said. "She said it was raspberryade."

"And that's all it was," the boy told him. "Harmless raspberryade."

"Right then." The lady in green stopped on the third floor, and Charlie was starting to get the feeling that each house had its own floor. "I am Professor Gone of the House of Sage." There was a little giggle which she ignored. "Inside you will find a small paper with just one question on it. You will enter the room in silence, answer the question in silence and then, and only then, when everyone, and I mean everyone, is finished and the papers collected will you be allowed to talk. There is a time limit, but we'll see how things go."

Up until that moment Charlie had been adamant he wanted to be in the House of Sage, but if it was all written tests like normal school, he thought he'd much rather be in Violet or Camellia.

The children shuffled into the room and Charlie's worst fear was realised. The room was just like the hall at primary school where they'd sat and done their SATs. Row upon row of individual desks were placed exactly fifty centimetres away from each other and on each desk was a piece of paper and a pen.

"Alphabetically please."

Charlie headed to the back of the room and found a desk with his name written in gold glowing on the desk. How on earth did they know he would be here? He looked around the room and there weren't any empty seats. Everyone was seated exactly where they should be. The names were different colours though, some gold like Charlie's, some green and some black.

"You may begin."

There was a rustling noise as everyone turned over their paper, the odd sigh or even a laugh as they read the problem they had to solve. Charlie's name was already written neatly on the top in what appeared to be his own handwriting and, sure enough, when he wrote it again underneath just to make sure he wasn't seeing things, it was an exact replica.

Professor Gone and the two prefects roamed around the room, walking up and down each aisle. As far as Charlie could see not one person had actually written an answer yet or even picked up their pen. From his vantage point at the back, he could see that most people were just staring at the paper in front of them or leaning nonchalantly back in their chair.

"Is there a problem, Mr Woods?" the professor asked, startling Charlie slightly as he was sure she'd been at the front of the room a second ago.

"Er … no, Professor." He turned his head away and concentrated on reading the question.

'Your dog walks for one hour at a speed of five miles an hour. His house is three miles away, and the shop is two miles away. Mandy lives in Watling Street which is five miles away and the vets is ten miles away. What's the name of the dog's owner?' Charlie looked at the question. Surely that couldn't be right? He read it again. How on earth was he going to answer that?

CHAPTER 12

He read the question for a third time before writing Mandy as the answer. As soon as he did this a second paper appeared on his desk with the same question. Charlie wrote Mandy once again and this time another piece of paper appeared again with the same question on. Five times he did this before stopping and sitting back in his chair.

Tasha was on the front row and Charlie could see she was frantically scribbling and then sobbed as another piece of paper appeared on her desk. A couple of desks were already empty so Charlie knew these children must have got the answer correct and were now members of the House of Sage.

A cry of horror came from the middle of the room, and Charlie watched as the pupil seemed to be swallowed up by a sea of paper but not one piece spilled out on to the other desks.

"I can see we are going to have to call an end to this soon." Professor Gone checked her watch after what felt like hours to Charlie. "Poor pickings for the House of Sage this year." She tutted as a tenth piece of paper appeared on the desk of the girl in front of her. "Miss Mills, I really did expect much better of you. Read the question." The girl's body seemed to collapse at her desk, and then, as if lightning had struck, she straightened herself up, wrote something on the paper and vanished into green smoke.

"Hallelujah!" the professor said and continued walking around the room.

Charlie looked back at his piece of paper. Perhaps everyone had a different question? Maybe that was part of the test but when he sneaked a peek at the boy's question next to him it appeared to be exactly the same.

A loud ticking sound disturbed the silence and a small clock appeared on everyone's desk. It was going backwards counting down rather than up, and Charlie started to panic as he realised there was now only fifty seconds left.

'Read the question.' The professor's voice rang in his head as more green smoke took pupils away. 'Your dog walks for one hour at a speed of five miles an hour.' Forty seconds. 'His house is three miles away, and the shop is two miles away.' Thirty seconds. 'Mandy lives in Watling Street which is five miles away and the vets is ten miles away.' Twenty seconds. 'What's the name of the dog's owner?' Ten seconds.

Charlie's head was throbbing, he couldn't think.

"Time's up everyone." The professor called. "Pens down."

"Charlie!" Charlie hadn't realised he'd shouted quite so loudly until the whole of the room turned to look at him.

"Quite correct, Mr Woods," the professor agreed. "But out of time, I'm afraid."

"How can it be Charlie?" the boy next to him asked.

"It's Charlie for me, but for you it would be…" He paused to read the black writing on the boy's desk. "…Kieran."

"I still don't get it." Kieran rubbed his head.

"Your dog walks for one hour." Charlie repeated the question with the emphasis on YOUR. "What's the name of the dog's owner? It's your name because it's your dog."

Kieran looked at him for a few seconds before he finally worked it out and a ripple followed around the room to the remaining students.

"Lovely to see you all again." It was Professor Brittle who now stood before them all, and instead of being in the room full of desks they were now back in the library with all the other students that had been there at the beginning of the day. Charlie hadn't seen any smoke or experienced that spinning feeling so he didn't know how they'd all got there.

The only thing that was different from this morning was that everyone was now grouped in their houses.

The House of Oak stood at the front with Professor Bones and his two prefects. Sandeep and Teddy waved to Charlie, but Bella turned her face away.

Zoe stood in the House of Violet right next to Mrs White.

Edward, Becky and the other Park Hill student smiled at them all from their place in the House of Camellia.

Alide and Chelsea were the happiest Charlie had ever seen them. They were holding hands and standing right at the back of the House of Borage. Professor Peculiar was still fighting with her wriggling hat.

Charlie wasn't quite sure who had joined the House of Sage but his question was answered when he saw Phoebe, Will and Tasha chatting away with the two prefects.

So that just left a small group of children, including Charlie, Dom and Daniel.

"It's been such an exciting day for all of us here and I know that many of you will have lots of questions for us so don't be frightened to ask your head of house or your prefects or one of the many members of staff around." Professor Brittle addressed them all from the front of the stage. "Most of you will return home to the NUM world and I'm afraid that is how it must remain for the next five years until you graduate." There was that NUM word again. "Some of you are lucky enough to have older siblings that have already graduated and will return to a SUM existence."

SUM? Charlie asked himself.

"And the very lucky amongst you will return home this evening to a whole new world of magic."

"Please, sir?" Charlie couldn't go on any longer without knowing and seeing as he didn't have a head of house to ask, he put his hand up.

"Yes, Charlie?" Professor Brittle, all the children and staff, in fact the entire library turned to look at him.

"If you don't mind me asking." He suddenly felt very small and stupid but determined to know the answer. "What's a NUM?" He paused. "And a SUM, come to mention it?"

Some of the children in the room giggled but most nodded in agreement with Charlie and looked towards Professor Brittle for the answer.

"Has no one explained that to you?" Charlie shook his head. "What a scatter-brained bunch we are today." There was a chiming noise from inside the professor's pocket again. He acted flustered, pulling out a gold fob watch. "Well, we'll have to answer that next week for you, Charlie. Now off you all go back to your floors. There's only another hour left before we need to get you all back in the elevator and off home. Your heads will have letters for you to take back and explain the various necessaries to you all." And with that he vanished into his gold cloud, and all the other houses vanished into their respective colours of smoke. Other members of staff walked out of the doors, and a few even shot up in the air and through the doors in the books.

"What do we do now?" Dom looked at Charlie, then Daniel, and then at the other eighty or so children. The room was empty and in darkness.

"Why you follow me, of course." A voice from the very top of the room called to them and, as they looked up, they could just see an old man waving at them from the door in the ceiling.

CHAPTER 13

"Who is that?" Daniel squinted his eyes.

"Haven't a clue." Dom replied.

"How do we even get up there?" one of the other children asked.

"Look!" Charlie pointed. "There's a ladder." It hadn't been there before, he was certain of it, but now right in front of them and leading directly up to the door was a gold ladder. It wasn't very wide but seemed sturdy enough as they all started to climb.

Charlie reached the top about halfway through the group and found himself inside rather a small office. It was so small that he wasn't sure how the eighty odd pupils that were left were going to fit. But fit they did and with room to spare. It was as if with every extra child that came in, the walls moved a little and the room expanded.

"Welcome to my office, everyone." The voice sounded familiar but although his clothes were those of Professor Brittle, the long grey hair, straggly beard and wrinkled face were not. "Sit down, sit down. Lots to talk about." Everyone sat down on the floor which was surprisingly soft and comfortable.

"Now then. I'm sure you all know by now which house you're in, and I've got all your letters here for you to take home." He waved a pile of papers at them.

"Excuse me, sir." A bespectacled girl near the front asked. "Who are you?"

"What do you mean 'who am I'?" He looked taken aback. "Where have you been all day?" He smoothed a hand through his hair. "Goodness me, not again." He pulled out the gold watch and tapped it gently. "Really need to get a new one of these." He tapped it again. "Quite rare though, long trip needed to find one." He tapped it again. "There we go." The long hair grew back into his scalp and turned brown and the lines smoothed from his face. The straggly beard shortened back to stubble on his chin.

"Professor Brittle!" the children chimed.

"Who else?" He smiled.

"So does this mean we're in your house?" Charlie asked. Could it be possible?

"The House of None welcomes you." Professor Brittle handed out two letters to each child, one was addressed to them the other to their parent or guardian. "Now, you are here because—"

"Excuse me, sir?" Daniel put his hand up, and Charlie noticed a few others including Dom and

Kieran were looking slightly bewildered. "I don't have a letter."

"Really?" He looked around the room and counted the faces before him. "Then you shouldn't be here." He pulled out his wand, flicked it, and over twenty children disappeared in puffs of gold. "Well, I don't know how that happened. I'm really going to have to look into these tests next year."

"Sir?" After everything he'd seen that day, it was probably the instant dismissal of those children that shook Charlie up the most.

"No need to worry about them, Charlie." Professor Brittle placed his wand back in his pocket. "I've sent them to oblivion, that's all."

"That's what I'm worried about, sir." Charlie was a little bit afraid. "The prefects from Violet House said it was the worst kind of hell imaginable."

"And indeed it is, Charlie." He clicked his fingers and a black leather chair flew into the room and positioned itself at the exact moment the professor chose to sit down. "To live without magic, to become a NUM again, well, it doesn't bear thinking about." Professor Brittle shivered. "Still don't know what a NUM is, do you?" The entire room of children shook their heads. "NUM stands for No Understanding of Magic and SUM stands for Some Understanding of Magic."

"So that makes us FUMS then," a black-haired boy at the back called out, and everyone laughed.

"FUMS?" Professor Brittle wasn't laughing.

"Full Understanding of Magic." the boy explained, to which a few laughed but soon stopped after seeing the professor's face.

"We have no need of silly names, Johnny." Professor Brittle was deadly serious. "We are magicians!"

"So, what happens when you go to oblivion?" Charlie wasn't really sure he wanted to know.

"A living nightmare." The professor shook his head. "You forget all about magic."

"You mean you just forget you had magic?" Charlie stared at him. "You don't torture them or anything?"

"Goodness me no, Charlie." He laughed. "This isn't the dark ages, you know."

"But if you've forgotten you had magic…" Charlie spoke his thoughts out loud. "…it wouldn't matter, because you didn't know any better."

"I've never thought of it that way." He pulled his glasses out from the top of his waistcoat. "I suppose we should think of another name, really. I'm always doing that, you know, but oblivion has such a nice ring to it, don't you think?" The children just stared at him. "Anyway, open your letters."

Charlie opened the one addressed to him and began to read.

Dear Student,

You have been accepted into the House of None under the patronage of Professor Brittle.

The House of None is a very special house, and you were chosen because you showed many attributes beneficial to the other houses but lacked all of them that were specific to one.

As with the other first years, you will attend the academy every Thursday during term time with special events over the holidays and some weekends.

When you return to your high school, you will not mention Brittle's Academy or anything you have seen here today. The teachers and pupils at your school will assume you have been at normal lessons like the rest of them.

You will of course require a Brittle's Academy uniform which will be available from your school office. Just ask for the BAMU kit and the receptionist will know exactly what to do.

You do not require any other equipment as pupils are not permitted to use wands until at least their third year, when they have mastered some control, and everything else will be provided for you.

Please attend the academy promptly on Thursday at 8:45 via the secret entrance which will lead you to the elevator.

We look forward to many years of magic and very little mayhem.

The other children were screaming in excitement, but all Charlie could think about was how on earth he was going to tell his mum that he needed another uniform.

CHAPTER 14

The queue for the elevator was enormous. The line of children stretched all along the floating path through the gates into the courtyard. They had all been instructed to re-group in their high schools to make it easier and quicker to return home.

"Of course Oak was the obvious choice for me," Bella said, bragging.

"All you did was climb a tree," Phoebe stated. "Some of us have done that and more." She dabbed at the cut on her elbow then rolled her sleeve back down to cover it.

"It wasn't just about climbing the tree," Bella protested. "It was having the strength and courage to succeed."

"Yeah, but it was basically climbing a tree," Teddy joked. "And I did it first." The others laughed as he continued to tease Bella.

"How much longer?" Alide tapped her foot. Chelsea was further down the line with St. Agatha's. Though she didn't like leaving her friend, she was eager to be home now and knew that next week and every week they would get to spend the entire day together.

"Can you believe it though. I mean really believe it?" Edward looked around him in awe. "Magic is real. One day, we're going to be fully fledged magicians."

There were excited murmurs of agreement as they shuffled forward.

"You're very quiet, Charlie," Tasha observed. "What's the matter?"

"Just in shock with it all, I think." How could he tell them about his mum?

"Don't worry about your mum," Sandeep said. He'd been there when Charlie's mum picked him up from his birthday party last year. She had shouted at him for ripping his jeans. "You're still clean and undamaged." He slapped a consoling hand on his shoulder.

"But we need another uniform," Charlie said. "She'll go absolutely mental. I've already been threatened with my cousin's hand-me-downs, so I dread to think what's going to happen when she finds out."

"Nothing wrong with hand-me-downs." Will pulled at a loose thread on his blazer. "This was my brothers," he said proudly.

"My cousin is a girl," Charlie stated.

"Oh!" came Will's simple reply.

They shuffled forward again.

"You heard what Brittle said." Edward had already dispensed with formal titles. "When you get home, you might find your mum is one of the SUMs, or maybe even a full magician."

"I doubt that very much." This really did make him laugh. His mum a magician? Alex? They wouldn't be living in their little terrace house working 9-5 jobs if they were magicians.

"Park Hill!" a male voice called.

"That was quick," Zoe said as they realised they were now standing in front of the elevator.

"In you go." The doors to the elevator were already wide open and a tiny man dressed in a grey suit with red and gold stitching was standing to the side. He was a little taller than the height of the blue downward arrow and his hand was permanently poised over the button. "Haven't got all day, you know."

They clambered in and as soon as the doors shut behind them they heard the lift ping again. "Peterborough High." Then another ping. "Queen's Academy."

"We can't all be using the same one?" Phoebe looked up, a little worried another lift might suddenly come crashing down on them.

"It's a magic school," Alide said. "Anything can happen."

The lift doors opened but instead of being back in the science block, they were at the side of the school building. The bell rang to signal the end of the day just as they stepped out and the lift doors disappeared. There were shouts of goodbye and see you tomorrow as they walked off through the little wooden gate in various directions.

"Alright, Charlie," Daniel Foster said. "That science teacher's a right one, isn't she? Homework on our first day."

"Daniel?" Even though Professor Brittle had explained all about oblivion, Charlie had still been a little worried. "You're not dead then?"

"Dead?" He looked at him with a raised eyebrow. "You feeling okay?"

"Course I am." He recovered himself remembering what he'd been told about talking of the academy. "Been a long day. Meant to say tired."

"I'm about beat, I have to admit, but it was nice having you in maths and science and I can't believe you're in 7B with Jack and Sandeep. Lucky you, getting two of your mates. I've got Alide and Phoebe." He pulled a face. "Never mind, got to go. See you tomorrow."

"Yeah, see you tomorrow." So it was true, everyone else believed they'd spent the day at Park

Hill and had even shared classes together. *This is going to take some getting used to*, he thought to himself.

He was halfway home when a car horn startled him. Charlie turned to see Alex in the blue Jaguar.

"Good day?" he asked, ruffling his brother's hair as he got in the front seat.

"Yeah." Charlie muttered. "But I've got to have a special uniform." He handed the letter to Alex. "Will you just get it for me without telling mum?".

"Oh, I wouldn't worry about mum." Alex checked his blind spot, a knowing smile on his face.

"Is that you, Charlie?" his mum called from the kitchen.

"Charlie's got a letter, Mum." He couldn't believe this was the first thing Alex was telling her. "Needs a special uniform and everything."

"I knew it!" She rushed into the hallway and scooped Charlie up in her arms. "Both my boys in Brittle's Academy."

Charlie, who had been expecting a completely different reaction, was surprised to say the least.

"And in the House of None." She was already reading the letter.

"You know about Brittle's Academy?" He looked at his brother and then his mother, who both nodded.

"House of Sage myself." He pulled out a wand from his overall pocket and it glowed green.

"My boys." She hugged them both tightly.

"Well, things are certainly going to be different from now on," Alex joked as two giant chocolate milkshakes appeared out of thin air.

"I wonder if they've sorted the sizing out yet," their mum muttered, looking at the order form attached to the letter. "Alex's coat was practically useless, only lasted him two terms, and don't get me started on the shirts. Flimsy things." She headed off into the living room.

"But nice to know some things will stay exactly the same." Charlie laughed, grabbed a glass from the air and chinked it against Alex's. "Cheers!"

THE END

Thank you for choosing this book. If you enjoyed it, please consider telling your friends or leaving a review on Amazon, Goodreads or the site where you bought it. Word of mouth is an author's best friend and much appreciated.

ABOUT THE AUTHOR

L ily Mae Walters chose her pen name in honour of her beloved Grandparents who also star in the Josie James series.

She is married with two almost grown up children, and two huskies that are the inspiration behind Murphy and Asher in the books.

Lily Mae lives in Nuneaton, England and finds herself using local places and even her old school in her stories.

Family and friends mean the world to Lily Mae and many will find themselves popping up throughout the series.

Lily Mae also writes for adults under the name of Florence Keeling.

Twitter: @LilyMaeWalters1
             @KeelingFlorence

ALSO BY LILY MAE WALTERS

JOSIE JAMES AND THE TEARDROPS OF SUMMER

Josie James is an ordinary 13-year-old until something extraordinary happens during her summer holidays.

Whilst staying at her Great Grandmother's cottage in the country she finds herself swept into the cursed world of Suncroft where it is perpetual winter.

Her new friends believe she could be the Chosen One who it is foretold will lift the curse but there are more pressing matters.

The Teardrops of Summer—magical crystals that render the owner immortal—have been stolen. Along with her telepathic husky-dog Protector Asher and her new friends, Josie must race to find the Teardrops and prevent catastrophe for their world.

Amazon Reviews for Josie James and the Teardrops of Summer:

"Josie James and the Teardrops of Summer is a children's (Middle Grade) book but makes for brilliant reading for adults too!

The plot is fascinating, starting with Josie's introduction to magic, elves and another world and dealing with the problem of the missing Teardrops, whilst only setting the ball rolling on the bigger story of the cursed Suncroft and the Chosen One who is destined to reverse the curse.

I was totally and utterly hooked!

Josie is a fantastic character: strong, curious and quick to piece clues together. I already love Asher (her telepathic dog-Protector), even though he really only makes a couple of cameos here, and there are clearly still plenty of secrets to uncover from her new friends and acquaintances. I particularly want to know more about the mysterious healers who 'help' the Elders rule.

The writing is smooth and immersive, and I loved the colourful descriptions. The 'chocolate box' settings described gave me a real feeling of old-timey warmth and nostalgia which fitted perfectly with the characters and storyline.

Highly recommend this for all readers from age 7 or so upwards, boy or girl, who enjoy fantasy adventures packed with intrigue and magic. If you're anything like me, you will be thrilled to hear that book 2 is on its way, and book 3 is already underway … I'll keep you posted!

Josie saw her nan sitting on one of the benches by the rose arbour talking to someone. Leaning out of the window slightly, she could hear her voice, but was too far away to hear what she was saying. Then, out of the corner of her eye, she saw what looked like a pair of green eyes staring at her through the roses. She blinked in disbelief and when she looked back, they were gone."

–Review by Steph Warren of Bookshine and Readbows blog

"I don't always read middle grade, but when I do, I hope it is as good as Josie James and the Teardrops of Summer! If I had an 8-10 year old, I most definitely would share this with him or her. Even though it is aimed toward a younger crowd, as an adult I was sucked in and loved every second of it.

Josie is such a great protagonist. She is bold and determined, yet self-aware for a 13 year old. She read as a 13 year old, and I love that. Lily Mae Walters has created a very relatable and realistic cast of characters that feel real and feel as if they are the ages they are supposed to be. I think that is so important for middle grade novels, and this is done exceedingly well here.

The world building of Suncroft is fantastic. It's a story of stumbling upon a magical world inside our own, but it is a very unique world and one unlike anything I've read in recent memory. I'm a huge fan of the fantasy elements of this story intermingled with a mystery Josie James needs to solve. The pacing is great. The beginning of the book is a sort of slow burn, as you learn the characters and the worlds, and then picks up the pace at the end. I could not put this one down!

I highly recommend this middle-grade novel as something you can read with your children or read as an adult and be swept away into a magical world!" –Jessica Belmont

"JOSIE JAMES AND THE TEARDROPS OF SUMMER by Lily Mae Walters is a wonderful tale brimming with magic and mayhem, with an intelligent female character that will charm your socks off.

Josie James is an ordinary girl with ordinary problems but when she visits her grandmother's house in the countryside she finds herself caught up in an adventure like no other. With magical worlds hidden within our own, creatures of all different types, and a curse that needs to be lifted by the Chosen One, Josie and her new friends have their work cut out for them. For if Josie doesn't stop the Teardrops of Summer from getting into the wrong hands, it could be the end of everything that she has come to care for.

Very easy to read and suitable for all ages, JOSIE JAMES AND THE TEARDROPS OF SUMMER by Lily Mae Walters is a wonderful and entertaining story that will enchant all those who read it. I really enjoyed Josie's character and loved reading about a young, intelligent, compassionate girl who isn't afraid to be who she is and make a difference. The book is well-paced and there is never a dull moment from start to finish. Overall, this is a delightful, magical tale that will appeal to children and adults alike and is definitely worth popping on to your to-buy list." –Amazon Reviewer

"This was such a fun read–I loved it!!

This is an enchanting story that I can see appealing to both boys and girls. The plot is well developed, the storyline is great and the characters are excellent—everything in this book works together and it makes for a very exciting story and ultimately a fun read!

No hesitation in giving this one 5 stars—very highly recommended!!" –Donna Maguire

JOSIE JAMES AND THE VELVET KNIGHT

"For you to find the Velvet Knight, you must solve the riddles thrice." A mysterious hooded figure, known only as the Velvet Knight has appeared in the cursed village of Suncroft. No one knows who he is or what he wants but when he starts leaving riddles around the village, it is time for Josie to return to Suncroft for a second time.

With Asher, her faithful husky Protector by her side, Filan, a half elf, and her great grandad, will they be able to solve the clues in time and discover his identity?

The Velvet Knight is not the only one causing problems for Josie. Her rival for the position of the 'Chosen One' continues to grow stronger, and now he has a Protector of his own.

What does all this mean for Josie? Is she destined to lift the wintery curse of Suncroft or will another take her place as the 'Chosen One'?

Printed in Great Britain
by Amazon

84193649R00061